This
MOUSE❈WORKS
Classics Collection Storybook

belongs to

_____

Disney's Peter Pan

ISBN: 1-57082-046-5
10 9 8 7 6 5

The Darling family lived in London, in a big house with a backyard. Six of them lived in the house: Mr. Darling, Mrs. Darling and their children, Wendy, Michael and John. Then there was Nana, the children's nursemaid. Nana also happened to be a dog, but she took wonderful care of the children. She served them breakfast, gave them their medicine and tucked them in bed at night. She also looked after them when their parents went out for the evening. On one such night, Mr. and Mrs. Darling were planning to go out to the theater. That same night, Peter Pan decided to visit the house. And it wasn't his first visit, either.

But before Mr. and Mrs. Darling could go out, they had to get dressed. Mr. Darling was upset because he could not get his tie just right. Although he was quite a clever man, Mr. Darling sometimes had trouble with simple tasks, such as getting dressed. This night, he was even more upset because his children had drawn a picture of a treasure map on his shirt front. Luckily, Mrs. Darling had been able to get the chalk marks out.

Still, Mr. Darling shouted at his children and he even shouted at poor Nana, who hadn't done anything wrong. Not even Mrs. Darling could calm him down.

Meanwhile, Michael and John were playing with cardboard swords, pretending they were Peter Pan and Captain Hook.

"You thought you could escape, Peter Pan, but now I've got you," said John, as they jumped across the bed.

Mr. Darling called the story of Peter Pan "poppycock and fiddle-faddle," but the Darling children believed that he was real.

"You're getting too old for this nonsense," Mr. Darling told Wendy. "This will be your last night in the nursery. Tomorrow you move to your own room!"

Wendy was not happy to hear this. And the whole family was unhappy when Mr. Darling decided to tie Nana outside for the night.

After Nana was tied outside and the Darling children were tucked in bed and kissed goodnight, Mr. and Mrs. Darling left for the theater. Immediately after they left, Peter Pan slipped into the window of the nursery. It seemed that he had visited the nursery a few nights earlier. He liked to sit in the shadows and listen to the wonderful stories Wendy told her brothers. However, on his last visit, Peter had gotten separated from his shadow and Nana wouldn't give it back to him. Wendy was thrilled when she woke up and saw Peter leaping across the room, chasing after his shadow. But she wasn't thrilled when she felt a tug at her hair.

"Ouch! Who's doing that?" squealed Wendy.

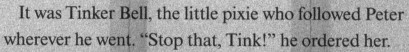

It was Tinker Bell, the little pixie who followed Peter wherever he went. "Stop that, Tink!" he ordered her.

When Peter finally caught his shadow, Wendy offered to sew it back on for him. He told her how much he liked listening to her stories.

"Yes, but I have to grow up tomorrow," she told him. "Tonight's my last night in the nursery."

"Come with me to Never Land," said Peter. "You'll never grow up there!"

Wendy thought Never Land sounded like a lot of fun, and she woke up Michael and John.

The boys couldn't wait to go to Never Land.

"But how will we get there?" Wendy asked.

"All you've got to do is fly," Peter told her.

The Darling children were astonished.

"But how do we do it?" said Wendy.

Peter scratched his head and thought. "All you have to do is think wonderful thoughts. And you need a little pixie dust, too!" He sprinkled pixie dust from Tinker Bell on them, and soon the Darling children were flying around the nursery.

"Come on. Let's go!" said Peter.

They flew all night long to
Never Land, an island
complete with a pirate cove,
an Indian village and a lagoon
where mermaids lived. They
could see Captain Hook's big
ship anchored in the bay.

Captain Hook had two
enemies: Peter Pan and a
hungry crocodile. One day,
while fighting with Peter, the
Captain had had his hand cut
off. The greedy crocodile had
grabbed the hand and
swallowed it. He liked the
taste so much, he had
followed Captain Hook ever
since, hoping to get another
tasty bite! Later, Captain
Hook had fed the crocodile a
clock. Then, at least, he
could hear the crocodile
sneaking up on him.

17

Captain Hook had very sharp eyes. As soon as he saw Peter Pan flying over the ship, he shouted, "Prepare for action! I'll get him this time! I've waited years for this."

Peter, Wendy and the boys were resting on a big cloud when Boom! There was a big explosion and the cloud was split in two by a cannonball shot from the ship.

"Tink, take Wendy and the boys to the island," said Peter Pan. "I must have a few words with my old friend, Captain Hook."

19

Tinker Bell agreed, but she had her own plan. She flew so fast, Wendy and the boys couldn't keep up with her. They could barely see her flying ahead of them. "Wait for us, Tinker Bell!" shouted Wendy.

Even though the Darling children flew faster than was safe for them, they couldn't even see the tiny flash of light from the pixie.

Tinker Bell had made up her mind that she didn't like Wendy, because the girl was taking Peter Pan's attention away from her. All she cared about was getting rid of Wendy. She dived down into a clump of trees on the island and headed straight for a hollow tree. She knew exactly where she was going and exactly what she would do.

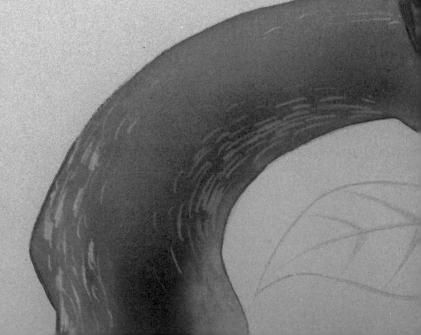

Tinker Bell flew into an opening in the tree where the Lost Boys lived. Peter was their leader and they were waiting for him to return from his trip to London.

"Hi, Tink! Where's Peter?" asked one of the boys.

Jingling and gesturing, Tink told the Lost Boys that there was a horrible bird flying toward them. It was called a Wendy Bird. She also told them that Peter had given them orders to "Smash it, kick it, shoot it!"

The boys went right into action, gathering up their slingshots and hurrying outside to capture the Wendy Bird for their leader.

When they saw Wendy and her brothers flying overhead, the Lost Boys aimed their slingshots and started shooting rocks at them. Wendy got hit by a big stone and was falling rapidly when Peter appeared just in time to catch her.

"Peter! You saved my life!" exclaimed Wendy, throwing her arms around Peter's neck. Tinker Bell was so jealous, she could hardly stand it.

"Is this how you welcome my friends!" said Peter to the boys. "I was bringing you a mother to tell you stories!"

The boys were ashamed of themselves. One of them spoke up. "But Tink said you wanted us to shoot the Wendy Bird down!"

Peter turned to Tink. "Is that true? Did you really lie to the boys?"

Tink didn't answer, but her face gave her away.

"Then you are banished from here – forever!" Peter said.

Even Wendy felt sorry for Tinker Bell. "Oh, Peter! Not forever," she said.

"Well, for a week, then," he agreed.

Peter introduced the Darling children to the Lost Boys, who
were very glad to have Wendy for a mother. Then, in order
to help her forget what had happened, Peter offered to take
her on a visit to Mermaids' Lagoon. Wendy was thrilled, for
she had never met a mermaid before.

Meanwhile, John led the Lost Boys and Michael in a
game of Follow the Leader, under waterfalls, over bridges
and across streams. Life in Never Land seemed to be one
long and delightful game.

But as the boys followed the
leader, they didn't know that
they were being followed as
well – by Indians! The Indians
didn't make a sound, but John
noticed something in the sand.
"Look! A footprint," he said.
  "A very big footprint,"
added one of the Lost Boys.

They didn't see an arrow
that whistled behind them and
landed in a tree. And they
didn't notice the eyes peering
at them from behind the
bushes. But they *did* notice
when the Indians jumped out
and grabbed them. The braves
carried the children back to
their camp.

Michael and John were very frightened when the Indians began to play tom-toms and sing war chants. The Lost Boys explained a game they played with the Indians. When the boys captured the Indians, they let them go. When the Indians captured the boys, they let *them* go.

"Not this time," said the Chief. "Where did you hide Princess Tiger Lily?"

The boys hadn't even seen the Indian princess, but the Chief wouldn't listen. "If Princess Tiger Lily is not back at sunset, you will burn at the stake!"

Meanwhile, Peter Pan and
Wendy had reached Mermaids'
Lagoon. "Oh, Peter! Just
imagine, real live mermaids!"
exclaimed Wendy.

Some of the beautiful
creatures were swimming in
crystal clear water. Others sat
on rocks, sunning themselves
or combing their long hair.
Peter introduced Wendy to the
mermaids. But the mermaids
were not glad to see Wendy.
Like Tinker Bell, they were
jealous of the girl.

One of the mermaids laughed at Wendy. "Look. She's wearing her nightgown," she giggled.

"Come on, leave her alone," Peter told them.

Suddenly, there was a strange noise.

"What is it, Peter?" asked Wendy.

"Pirates!" Peter whispered as they rushed to hide behind the cliff.

Captain Hook's first mate, Mr. Smee, was rowing a small boat. "It's Hook. He's captured Princess Tiger Lily! We've got to save her," Peter decided.

"Where are they going?" asked Wendy.

"It looks like they're taking her to Skull Rock," Peter explained. "There's no time to waste!"

Hiding inside the cove, Peter and Wendy saw the pirate
boat pass close by. There were three figures in the boat:
Hook, Mr. Smee and Tiger Lily. Her arms were tied. Peter
and Wendy listened carefully to what the pirates said.
Hook had brought the Indian Princess to the rock to die
when the tide rose.

Captain Hook gave Tiger Lily a choice. "Tell me the hiding place of Peter Pan and I shall set you free."

Tiger Lily listened, but she didn't say a word, so Hook continued. "If you won't tell us, we will have no choice but to leave you here. And you know what will happen then. The water will slowly rise − to your knees, to your arms, to your chest and finally to your head. And then it will be too late for you, Tiger Lily!"

Still, the Indian Princess did not say a word. Wendy was impressed that Tiger Lily was so brave, even in the face of death.

"Watch this, Wendy!" Peter Pan jumped in the air and landed on Hook's boat. When the pirate saw him, he was overcome with rage and pulled out his sword. But Peter was fast. He jumped on the blade and bounced up and down as if he were on a spring.

41

The fight that followed was fierce, and neither Peter nor
Hook would give in. "Blast you, Pan! I've got you now!"
snarled the pirate captain.

As Hook thrust his sword at the boy, Peter leaped from
rock to rock. "You haven't caught me yet," laughed
Peter.

Hook began fighting even harder. Just when he was
about to win the sword fight, Mr. Smee called out, "I
say, Captain, do you hear something?"

Sure enough, the tick-tock of the crocodile's clock was
moving toward Captain Hook.

"Smee! Help!" shouted the pirate as he lost his
balance. He found himself hanging by his hook, just above
the crocodile's open jaws.

"I'm coming, Captain, I'm coming! Hold on!" Smee was rowing as hard as he could, as Hook slipped down into the jaws of the hungry crocodile. With all his might, he fought the crocodile, but he knew he couldn't fight much longer.

"Now, Smee! Now!" shouted the terrified pirate. The crocodile's jaws were just about to snap shut.

While Hook was fighting for his life, Peter swam to
Tiger Lily and saved her just in time. All he could see
was a little feather pointing out of the water! "You must
have been scared to death," Peter said.

Tiger Lily thanked Peter for saving her life. Just as he lifted
her out of the water, they saw Mr. Smee rowing Captain Hook
back to the ship as fast as possible. The crocodile was
swimming right behind them. Wendy joined Peter and Tiger
Lily and they all flew back to the Indian village.

When they got to the village, the first thing they did was to greet Tiger Lily's father, the Big Chief. The Chief called Peter "Mighty Warrior" and made him an honorary Indian to thank him for saving his daughter's life. Then Peter and the Chief sat in the tepee and Peter wore a big feather-headdress.

The children were set free and joined in the festivities. As the Indians played the tom-toms, a dance was held around the totem pole.

Everyone had a wonderful time, except Wendy, who sat to one side, thinking that Peter hadn't paid any attention to her since he had saved Tiger Lily's life.

Wendy was relieved when Peter announced it was time to go home. John was the leader once again, and the Lost Boys sang as they followed him through the forest.

They were all feeling happy and triumphant. Little did they know that Captain Hook had a new plan to destroy Peter Pan. This time, he would use Tinker Bell to help him trap his enemy.

Hook had learned that Tink had been banished by Peter.

"Trap her, Smee," commanded the scheming Hook. "She may help us do what we want!"

Tinker Bell was still in exile and she still blamed Wendy for all her problems. She wanted revenge, but she hadn't come up with any ideas yet.

When Smee found the tiny pixie, he took off his cap and trapped her in it.

"Captain Hook would like to have a little chat with you," he chuckled.

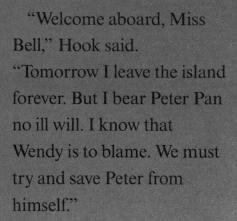

"Welcome aboard, Miss Bell," Hook said. "Tomorrow I leave the island forever. But I bear Peter Pan no ill will. I know that Wendy is to blame. We must try and save Peter from himself."

Tink was interested in what Hook had to say.

"We'll kidnap that girl until he comes to his senses. But we don't know where he lives," Hook told her.

Tink hesitated.

"After all, if I don't know where he lives, how can I find Wendy and get rid of her?" Hook asked.

This made a lot of sense to Tinker Bell.

Hook could hardly contain his glee as Tinker Bell pointed out Peter's hideout on the map.

"Thank you, my dear. You've been most helpful," said Hook. And then he burst into laughter. "Here's your reward," he sneered, as he grabbed Tinker Bell and locked her up in a lantern. Tink was trapped!

Meanwhile, in the hollow tree, all the Lost Boys gathered around Wendy. They listened carefully as she told them wonderful stories and sang them a song about mothers. Some of the boys had been away from home a long time and could barely remember their mothers, but suddenly they felt sad and longed to go home.

Some of the boys even cried at the sad stories. Just outside the tree, the pirates were getting ready to attack. But when they heard Wendy's stories, they stopped to listen. When Wendy sang about a mother's love, even the tough pirates could not help but cry, thinking about their own mothers, now so far away.

When Wendy finished, all the boys decided that they wanted to go back to their own mothers!

Peter was angry. "You can go, if you want. I'm not holding you here," he told them. "But I warn you, if you go back, you'll grow up and you'll never be able to return to Never Land!"

The Lost Boys didn't hesitate. It seemed to them that even growing up wouldn't be so bad if you had a mother to care about you. They all hurried up the stairs.

Wendy stayed behind to say goodbye to Peter. "You could come with us, too," she told him.

But Peter chose to stay in Never Land.

Although Wendy was sad to leave Peter, she was looking
forward to flying back home to London. But as soon as she
was outside, she discovered that all the boys had been captured
by the pirates. "Grab her and tie her up!" shouted one of them.
And Wendy was captured, tied up with thick ropes and carried
away through the dark forest.

"Captain Hook will be happy to see you," sneered one
of the pirates. Neither Wendy nor the boys knew what
their fate would be once they reached the pirate ship.

The pirates carried their prisoners onto the ship. "First we were captured by Indians and now we are captured by pirates," thought John. The pirates tied all the children to the big mast. Michael missed his teddy bear already.

"Whoever makes the first move will be in trouble," growled one of the pirates.

"Yo-ho for the life of a pirate," they all began to sing.

The boys trembled as they watched the pirates. Even when they danced, the big, rough pirates looked mean. "How will we ever get off this ship?" the children wondered.

Hook was seated at one end of the ship and all the pirates sang in chorus, lifting their skull-and-crossbones flags high in the air.

"Mr. Smee!" ordered Captain Hook. "Bring our captives here at once!"

"What will he do with us?" thought Wendy as she and the boys huddled together.

"Perhaps he'll set us free," Wendy thought.
Smee then announced that their lives would be spared on one condition: They would have to sign up and become pirates on Captain Hook's ship.
"Never!" said Wendy. "We won't do it."
"Then you'll have to walk the plank," snarled Hook.
"Peter will save us," said Wendy.

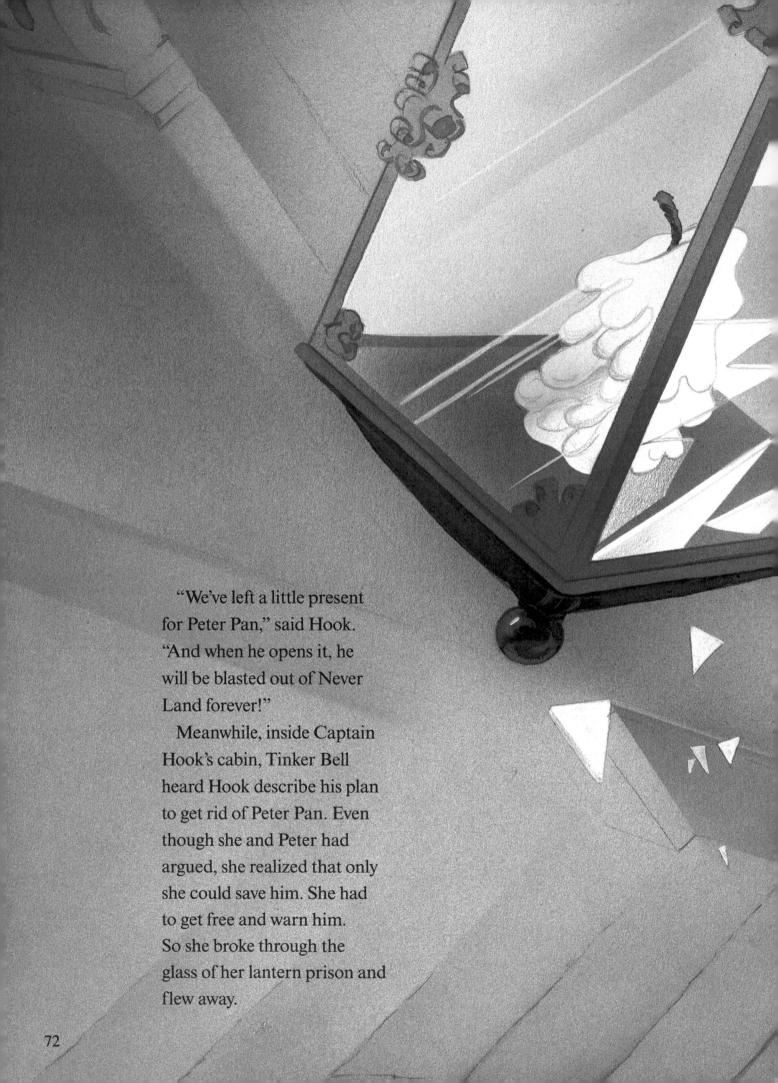

"We've left a little present for Peter Pan," said Hook. "And when he opens it, he will be blasted out of Never Land forever!"

Meanwhile, inside Captain Hook's cabin, Tinker Bell heard Hook describe his plan to get rid of Peter Pan. Even though she and Peter had argued, she realized that only she could save him. She had to get free and warn him. So she broke through the glass of her lantern prison and flew away.

Back in his hideout, Peter was playing his flute. Then, for the first time, he noticed the package that had been left there by the pirates. There was a little note on the present which read: "To Peter Pan, with love from Wendy."

Peter couldn't wait to see what was in the package. He could hear ticking inside, which made him feel even more curious.

Tink, who had flown as quickly as she could, was just in time to grab the package from his hands. She flew away with the heavy box as fast as she could.

Tink had just taken the package away from Peter when the bomb exploded!

Peter was not hurt, but at first, he could not find Tinker Bell. "Tink! Where are you?" he cried. Then he heard her tinkling sound. She was all right, after all!

"Tink, you mean more to me than anyone in the world," Peter told her.

But she was still worried. She told Peter that Captain Hook had kidnapped Wendy and the boys. There was no time to waste. The children would walk the plank unless Peter saved them!

Peter jumped up. "Let's go, Tink!" he said.

On the pirates' ship,
Captain Hook told the
children it was time to make
a decision. "What will it
be?" he asked. "Stay with us
and live the life of a pirate,
or take a trip to the bottom of
the ocean? What's your
choice?"

The boys might have been
tempted to become pirates,
but Wendy had decided
otherwise. "We prefer to
die," she told him. "Besides,
Peter Pan will save us, one
way or another." She bid her
brothers and the other boys
goodbye. Then, head held
high, she walked bravely out
onto the plank.

On the ship's deck, the boys and the pirates all held their breath. Then Wendy jumped and disappeared. But to the pirate's surprise, there was no sound of her hitting the water. "No splash!" Smee exclaimed.

"What did you say? No splash?" asked Hook. None of them knew that Peter had been hiding by the side of the boat. When Wendy had jumped, he had caught her in midair.

"Oh, Peter! I was sure you would come!" Wendy told him.

Peter helped Wendy to a safe place and then he leaped up onto the deck. Suddenly, Hook found himself face to face with Peter again. The others drew back, forming a circle around the two enemies.

"This time you've gone too far, Pan," cried Hook, drawing his sword. "Take that!"

Peter wasn't worried. He enjoyed a good fight with Hook. The pirate lunged forward, his sword pointing at Peter's heart. But the boy was quicker and smarter than Hook. Instead of piercing Peter, the blade stuck in the ship's mast.

"Get me another sword at once," demanded Hook. As soon as he was handed another sword, he lunged at Peter again, but Peter leaped into the air to escape the blow. Peter darted and hopped all over the ship without showing any sign of getting tired.

His speed and agility were so confusing to Captain Hook, the pirate lost his balance.

Hook was perched on the ship's rigging. When he looked into the water below him, he saw a terrible sight. The crocodile had been watching the sword fight and waiting, hoping to get another taste of the pirate. The captain screamed in terror when he saw the hungry creature. Then he slipped and went flying through the air, down, down, down.

This time, there *was* a splash!

"Hurray for Captain Pan!" shouted the boys on deck. Below, they could see Mr. Smee rowing the other pirates away in a small boat. Captain Hook was swimming furiously behind the boat with the crocodile in pursuit.

"Hurry up. We're casting off!" shouted Peter.

"Where are we going?" asked Wendy.

Peter smiled broadly. "I'm taking you back to London!"

"Go ahead, Tink!" he ordered.

As the children cheered, Tinker Bell sprinkled golden pixie dust all over the ship!

What happened next was most unusual, even in Never Land. The boat, which had become a beautiful glowing golden color and grown as light as a feather, was carried up by the wind. It could be clearly seen sailing proudly across the sky.

It floated high above the bay and the forest. The Indians couldn't believe their eyes when the ship drifted overhead.

The ship sailed effortlessly for a very long time. Suddenly, Michael cried out, "Did you hear it?"

"Hear what?" his sister asked.

"Big Ben ringing from the Westminster clock!" he answered happily. "We're home again!"

When Mr. and Mrs. Darling returned home, they found their three children asleep in the most surprising places. Wendy was on the window sill. Michael was lying at the foot of his bed and John was asleep on the floor, holding his top hat on his chest.

As their parents tried to put them back in their beds, the children awoke and began to chatter excitedly of their wonderful adventures in Never Land.

"Peter Pan took us there and we met the Lost Boys. Then we were taken prisoner by the Indians and after that by the pirates, but Peter saved us both times," Wendy said.

Mr. Darling didn't pay any attention to her. "I guess we'll have to wait awhile before you're grown up. And it seems we need Nana in the nursery, after all," he said, bringing the dog inside.

Suddenly, out of the window, they could see the shadow of a big ship cast over the moon. "Look! That's Peter's ship. He's going back to Never Land!" John exclaimed.

And as he watched, Mr. Darling said, "You know, I have the feeling that I've seen that ship before. But it was a long time ago, when I was very young."